SWAMP FURIES

ANNE SCHRAFF

SADDLEBACK
PUBLISHING • INC.

TAKE TEN NOVEL SERIES

Disaster

Sports

Mystery

Adventure

Project Editor: Liz Parker
Cover Designer and Illustrator: Marjorie Taylor
Text Illustrator: Fujiko Miller

© 1992 Saddleback Publishing, Inc.

SADDLEBACK
PUBLISHING • INC.

3505 Cadillac Ave., Building F-9
Costa Mesa, CA 92626

ISBN 1-56254-056-4
Printed in U.S.A.
3 4 5 6 7 8 M 99 98 97 96 95

Chapter 1

Shane Shay liked the idea of spending the summer on Captain Thunder's old bayou houseboat. Shane was sixteen and this would be his first good job. Besides, he loved the bayou.

"But old Captain Thunder is sort of a bum," Dad argued. "I'm not sure I want you working for him."

"And there are alligators in the bayou," Mom said. "What if the rotten old boat sinks?"

"Don't worry," Shane told his parents. "We go out at ten in the morning. We'll be back at six in the afternoon. I'll just bike down and home every day. It'll be easier than going to school!" And lots more fun, Shane thought. And the money! Finally his parents agreed. So now, with a few puffy clouds in the blue Louisiana sky, Shane pedalled the short distance to Crayfish bayou.

Shane saw Captain Thunder on the houseboat as he rounded the last bend. Captain Thunder took off his greasy old cap and waved it at Shane. Shane waved back. An excited grin spread over Shane's face. He really enjoyed Captain Thunder's tall tales about wrestling alligators and seeing Captain Kidd's ghost rising from the swamps! He liked the Blackbeard headless ghost story best.

"Shane, I want you to meet the nice folks going with us today," Captain Thunder said. "These nice ladies are Mabel and Ethel Stanton, retired school-teachers from Cleveland, Ohio."

Shane smiled at the two blue-haired ladies. They looked around wide-eyed at the cypress trees and the oak trees hung with Spanish moss. "This is the

first time we've ever been in Louisiana," Mabel, the taller of the two, said.

"Nice to meet you," Shane said. They reminded him of his Spanish teacher.

"And here's the Cochran family," the Captain said.

Tom Cochran was big with a red face. Janet, his wife, was pretty with golden hair. Little Robbie was eight. He tried to kick Shane in the shins, but Shane stepped out of the way just in time. Shane didn't like little Robbie very much.

"Ready to shove off, folks?" Captain Thunder shouted. "The gators are waiting on us—the swamp calls!"

The Stanton sisters giggled. Janet Cochran smiled up at her husband, and Robbie said, "Do the gators eat people, Captain Thunder?"

Captain Thunder gave Robbie a wicked smile. "That they do, lad. They live for the pure delight of eating folks.

They like certain things more than others, like people do, don'tcha see? And nothing is so tempting to a hungry gator as a small red-haired boy."

Shane laughed hard at the joke. The Cochrans seemed a little bit angry, but Robbie just said, "Betcha the gator eats you before he eats me, Captain Thunder."

"Not a chance, laddie. My whiskers would tickle his great green throat!" Captain Thunder snorted.

Shane helped the Stanton ladies settle into their deck chairs. Then he returned to the stern so Captain Thunder could show him how to steer the boat.

"You're a smart lad, and she's easy to handle," Captain Thunder said.

Shane took a turn and got the wooden boat safely past stands of blue hyacinths and duckweed.

"Thatta boy," Captain Thunder said heartily. He excused himself for a brief trip down to his cabin and returned a little shaky on his feet. Shane shuddered. They were barely underway and already Captain Thunder was drinking!

Chapter 2

"Now listen up, folks," Captain Thunder said in a slurred voice, "and learn the terrors of the swamp!"

"I want to hear a pirate story," Robbie yelled. "I want to hear a pirate story about bloody heads and stuff like that. And skeletons."

"I'd like to bloody *your* head, mate," Captain Thunder muttered softly. Luckily, nobody but Shane heard it. In a louder voice, Captain Thunder said, "When I was a wee lad, a terrible storm came to this bayou. The water was sucked right out of the sky. Then she came crashing down. Aye ... hundreds were drowned like rats. And the moon, she lay in the bayou and we thought it was the end of the world."

Mabel Stanton cleared her throat and said, "I'm sure you mean that the reflection of the moon was in the bayou."

"Hush, Mabel," short, chubby Ethel Stanton whispered. "We're retired from school teaching, remember."

"Did the gators eat the moon?" Robbie asked.

A huge white swamp bird screeched suddenly, sending a shiver up Shane's spine.

"No, laddie," Captain Thunder said, staggering towards the boy, "but the gators ate plenty of folks that day. The folks were tossed into the bayou, don'tcha see? And, aye, the gators had themselves a feast. Ate the folks head first, slurp, slurp, SLURP!" At the last loud slurp, Captain Thunder's face was inches from Robbie's.

"You smell funny!" Robbie shrieked, backing away. Shane hurried to the rescue. He figured the boy was smelling the whisky on Captain Thunder's breath.

"Come on, Robbie," Shane said, taking Robbie's arm, "I'll even let you steer, okay?"

Robbie pulled away from Shane and aimed a kick at Shane's shins. Robbie was wearing expensive cowboy boots, and Shane yelled in pain.

"Oh, dear," Janet Cochran said. "Mustn't kick, darling." Then she looked sternly at Shane, "My son doesn't like to be touched. So please don't try to take his arm like that again, Shane. Okay?"

Shane felt his face burn with fury. He wanted to grab the brat and give him a good shake. But they were Captain Thunder's customers. Shane worked for Captain Thunder. So Shane smiled through gritted teeth and said, "Yes, ma'am. Sorry."

"Tell us a good story, Captain Thunder," Robbie said. "I want to hear about a bloody pirate or a ghost."

Captain Thunder glared at the boy but he said, "Why, Blackbeard's beheaded body sank right in this very bayou. His headless ghost is around and about. When the weather is just right, you can see it. The headless Blackbeard floats on the water like a boat. By the light of the moon it glows. They say old Blackbeard is swimming around, looking for his head...."

"That's a good story," Robbie said. He took a small water pistol from his back pocket. Shane hoped he wouldn't be such a fool to shoot a spout of water at Captain Thunder.

Captain Thunder went on, "When a strong wind blows, like now, why folks can hear Blackbeard's ghostly voice. 'Where's me head?' he cries, 'where's me head?'"

When Captain Thunder turned for another trip to his cabin, Robbie aimed the water pistol and shouted, "There's me head! There's me head!"

The blast of water got Captain Thunder in the back of his head. His grayish white mane of hair was soaked. He spun around, fury in his eyes.

Chapter 3

Shane got between Captain Thunder and Robbie, "Calm down," Shane whispered. "The little brat's gonna get what he deserves—*someday!*"

Captain Thunder hurried down to his cabin, and Shane turned to the stern. As he steered the boat, he shouted to the passengers, "Let's have a little sing-along until Captain Thunder comes back. Let's see—

'Yo-ho, blow the man down,
Yo-ho, the bend's coming 'round!'"

"I hate singing," Robbie said. "I want to hear another ghost story. I want to hear how Captain's alligators get fed."

"We feed them raw chicken legs,"

Shane said.

"Yuk," Robbie said with a toothless grin.

"I read somewhere that alligators are quite gentle." Mabel said. "They can be trained like a dog."

Shane didn't know as much as Captain Thunder about the bayou, but he knew a lot for a sixteen-year-old. "No ma'am," he said. "Alligators will come to the side of the boat if a familiar voice yells that it's chow time. They jump up for the chicken, but you don't want to be thinking they're tame. They have powerful jaws. Can bite a leg off real easy."

"All right!" Robbie shouted.

As the canopied boat moved smoothly deeper into the swamp, Shane pointed out cabbage palms and black-eyed Susans. They passed an old abandoned plantation house. Old cypress trees stood around it with trunks like gray and white marble. A giant oak, its

branches dripping with Spanish moss, stood near the rotting porch.

"I imagine there's a story there," Mabel said. "I'm something of a Civil War buff. Most of the old houses have a tragic tale to tell if they only could speak."

Shane had been around Captain Thunder since he was five or six. He was a troubled old fellow, but Shane liked him. And Shane had picked up a lot of Captain Thunder's tricks of the trade. Now Shane smiled and said, "Yep, there's a story there all right. It's a ghost story, too."

It didn't matter if such stories had any truth in them. Captain Thunder taught Shane that. It was something to entertain the passengers with. It was part of the adventure of gliding down the bayou under a pale, greenish sky.

"A pretty girl named Desiree lived in that mansion. A handsome fellow named Rene Depre wanted to marry her. But then he changed his mind. Desiree was so mad she tried to push Rene into the river. But she fell in instead. Now their ghosts both go moaning through the house. They're looking for each other. But being ghosts, why, they just never will get together," Shane said.

"How sad," Mabel said.

"That's a dumb story," Robbie snorted.

Shane never saw Captain Thunder come up from the cabin. Shane knew that once Captain Thunder nursed a wounded baby alligator back to health, and now and then he'd pull the gator on the boat. He'd do it to amuse and amaze the passengers. But now he fished his friendly alligator from the bayou for another reason.

When Shane turned, he saw the alligator lumbering towards the deck chairs.

"Eeeeee," screeched the Stantons.

Captain Thunder had drunk way too much. He was laughing like a madman as he herded the confused little alligator along. The alligator's mouth was wide open. Shane knew the young alligator wouldn't do anybody any harm, but Robbie didn't know it. And Captain Thunder was herding the gator right for the boy. "Git 'em, baby!"

Chapter 4

Tom Cochran scooped up his screaming son, and Janet fainted into the arms of Mabel Stanton. Ethel Stanton was waving her umbrella at the alligator and saying, "Scat! Scat, you bad alligator!"

Captain Thunder howled with laughter as he got a noose and slipped it around the alligator. He spilled the alligator back into the bayou. Then he shouted at the boy, "That'll teach you to shoot water spouts at Cap'n Thunder, ye little devil!"

Tom Cochran glared at the drunken captain. "I shall see that you lose your license for this, you beast!"

"Aww, shut your big, flapping

mouth," Captain Thunder shouted. He was taking swigs from his bottle now without shame. "You ought to thank me for scaring some manners into your little cockroach of a boy!"

The Stanton sisters had fanned Janet Cochran back to consciousness. She rose up like a tornado. "My baby," she screamed, grabbing Robbie and hugging him. "He tried to feed my baby to a horrible alligator. That monster! I demand that he go to jail!"

"Just calm down," Shane pleaded. Captain Thunder had gone too far, that was for sure. He never would have done such a thing if he were sober. For the first time since they set off on the bayou, Shane was sorry he'd signed on. Dad was right. You can't put your trust in a drinking man! And now here they were, in the middle of the bayou with a war underway!

"Mr. Cochran, please calm your wife down. Captain Thunder was just joking.

That's sort of a tame gator, see. It's like at the parks, you know, where the fake animals threaten the tourists just for fun."

Mabel Stanton said, "But you said there were no tame alligators, young man."

Great! Shane thought. Just what he needed. Mabel reminding him of the stories he'd told!

"I will not calm down," Janet cried. "I want that evil man put in chains!"

"Ma'am," Shane said, "we're out in the middle of nowhere and we have one Captain to get us safely home, so will you please be quiet?"

"I most certainly will *not* be quiet," Janet shrieked louder than the sea birds. "Thomas, it's up to you to make a citizen's arrest of the Captain."

Tom Cochran moved towards Captain Thunder.

"You put your clammy hands on me, mate, and I'll break you in two and

throw half of you to the gators on the left side of the boat and the other half to them on the right side of the boat," Captain Thunder yelled.

Tom Cochran turned to Shane, "Come on, young fellow, we'll go at him together."

Shane was a tall, strong young man, but he wasn't about to take on Captain Thunder. "You guys!" Shane cried, "just let the whisky wear off, and Captain Thunder will be okay!"

In two seconds Captain Thunder clambered over the side like a monkey. He plunged into the bayou and began swimming.

"You won't escape justice!" Janet Cochran screamed after him.

Captain Thunder turned and took a last look at the rotten boat. "The devil take ye all!" he bellowed before skimming through the water like a fish. He scrambled onto shore and vanished like a ghost into the cypress swamp.

"Thank goodness!" Janet Cochran said. "When we get back we'll send the sheriff after him."

Shane felt cold. Just as Captain Thunder jumped, the boat hit a sharp rock in the swamp. The boat was taking water.

Chapter 5

"Don't everybody scream at once," Shane said, "but this houseboat is heading for the bottom of the bayou!"

The Cochrans turned as pale as oysters and clung to each other. Robbie began to sniffle. The Stanton sisters stared at Shane hopefully.

"Can you do something?" Mabel asked.

"You *must* do something," Ethel snapped in her teacher voice.

Shane steered the boat towards shore, hoping they'd get to land before the houseboat tilted too badly and spilled everybody into the swamp. Shane tried not to glance into the murky water. It was filled with alligators. They'd sun themselves in the grass, then splash into deep water if they smelled food.

"Hang on to the railing," Shane shouted to his frightened passengers. "Don't anybody slip over!" It dawned on Shane then with a jolt. *He* was the captain of this sinking ship! He was the leader of this doomed tour! He was sixteen years old, and they were all looking to him to be saved!

With a shudder the old houseboat plunged through some water lilies and ran into some vines. "I think this is as far as we go," Shane said.

"You mean we have to wade through that scummy swamp to get to shore?" Janet Cochran demanded.

"It's not deep, ma'am," Shane said.

Now that the danger of going down with the boat had passed, Robbie was excited again. "Are there blood suckers in the water? I read in a comic book how blood suckers stick to your skin and *suuuck*—"

"Robbie darling, please!" Janet groaned, clutching her head.

Shane got a rope and tied everyone loosely together for the trip through the shallow water. "In case somebody slips, we can all pull you back up," he said, trying to sound cheerful. "Sometimes there's a suck hole that takes you right down."

"Does it suck you to the bottom of the ocean where the octopus lives?" Robbie demanded.

"No," Shane said. He amused himself for a minute by picturing an octopus hugging Robbie. This was all the kid's fault. Captain Thunder wouldn't have freaked out if the kid hadn't shot the water pistol at him.

Shane led the way down from the sinking boat to the swamp. The Stanton sisters followed, with the Cochrans bringing up the rear.

"I'll carry you, son," Tom Cochran

reached for his son.

"No!" Robbie cried. "I want to wade in the slime!"

"You'll get all wet and dirty, dar-ling," Janet said. "Should I carry you, darling? Mommy will carry ..."

"No!" Robbie spit out the words. He was getting red in the face. "I won't be carried like a baby!"

Shane wanted to say, "Oh, let him sink to the bottom and get eaten by the crabs." But instead he said, "Just hang on to the boy, folks. It safe enough for him to walk."

The Stanton sisters wore long slacks, but Janet wore shorts. It wasn't long be-fore a slippery diving beetle swished across her bare ankle. "Eeeech!" Janet screeched, "Some hideous giant, dis-gusting insect is attacking me!"

"Take it easy," Shane said. "It's just a beetle. They don't harm anybody."

"Can I catch one?" Robbie asked, stooping to stare into the cloudy swamp. "Maybe I can keep it alive un-til we get home! Hey look! A big red snake's down here!"

Chapter 6

"Coral snake!" Ethel Stanton cried in alarm. "They're red and yellow and deadly! Run! Everybody run!"

"No!" Shane shouted, stopping the mad stampede. "It's just an old blood worm!"

"A blood worm? Neato!" Robbie shouted. "Do they suck blood?"

"Come on, you guys," Shane shouted, hurrying the group forward. In another minute they were scrambling onto the spongy earth. A clump of dead trees lay ahead, filled with buzzing and chirping sounds. A gray kingfisher dove arrow-like into the water for a fish.

"Whew," Shane said when they

were on fairly solid ground. "We made it!"

"I'm hungry," Robbie said. "When are we gonna eat?"

Shane remembered that Captain Thunder said the four-hour boat ride would end at a little Cajun diner on the river. That was a *long* way off.

"I've got some grain and raisin bars in my knapsack," Shane said.

"Yuk!" Robbie grunted, wrinkling his nose.

"It'll have to do until we get out of here," Shane said. He passed out two bars to each in the group. Robbie promptly threw his two bars at a great blue heron nesting in a nearby tree.

"Okay for you, kid," Shane snapped, losing his temper, "but don't expect anybody to share if you get good and hungry!"

"Don't yell at the boy," Tom Cochran said sharply, "he's only a child. He's scared enough without you yelling at him."

"Look," Shane said, growing angrier by the minute, "we'll get out of this okay, I hope, but we have a *serious* problem. The swamp is dangerous, and we can't be putting up with the mischief of some spoiled brat!"

The Cochrans glared silently at Shane. Shane heard them muttering between themselves, calling Shane a "nasty punk." Shane ignored them and looked for a fairly good path through the trees. He planned to head for the old plantation house about a mile away. He figured he could leave the tourists there and then run through the swamp to the ranger station. He knew the ranger. He'd haul everybody out in a swamp buggy. That was the plan anyway.

The trail was overgrown with vines, and Shane had to stop frequently and cut a path. Birds shrieked from the oak trees, which were almost smothered in

Spanish moss.

"Look at the pirate beards," Robbie said.

Mabel smiled at the boy and said, "That's Spanish moss, isn't it, Shane? But it does look like a beard."

"I wanna climb a tree and get some," Robbie said.

Shane turned and yelled, "No!" He didn't care anymore if the Cochrans were mad at him or not. The summer job with Captain Thunder was gone. A whole fun summer of riding the bayou and making money was ruined. Poor old Captain Thunder would get sober and remember what he'd done—that he'd almost drowned his passengers and sunk his boat. He'd probably hide in the swamp for the rest of his life! He'd join the other ghostly creatures living in the swamp, the snow-white birds and the prowling pirates.

A vine almost knocked Mabel Stanton down, and as Shane was helping her, Robbie began exploring. Nobody noticed until Janet cried, "Where's Robbie?"

"He was trying to poke some Spanish moss down with a stick when I saw him last," Ethel said.

"Robbie! My darling! Where are you?" Janet screamed.

Chapter 7

"Oh boy, this is great!" Shane grumbled. "Now we have to look for a lost kid! Why didn't you guys hang onto him?"

"He's curious," Tom Cochran said. "Is that a crime? He's an active little boy. He *must* be around here somewhere. Robbie! Come out if you're hiding."

"Robbie, darling," his mother called, "I know you're playing hide-and-seek behind a tree. But you're making Mommy and Daddy upset. Come out, darling. When we get back to town we'll buy you a double-decker ice-cream cone if you come out right away."

"Oh, brother!" Shane growled, searching the low branches of the trees for some sign of the boy. Robbie was wearing a green t-shirt and jeans. Everything in the swamp was gray or green except for the birds and the butterflies, which were brightly colored.

The towering trees were so choked with creeping vines that an army could have been hidden in their branches.

"Robbie Cochran," said Mabel Stanton in her sharpest teacher voice, "you come out this minute." Mabel used to teach in a private school, where all of the children had pretty good manners.

"Robert Cochran," Ethel said in an even sharper voice, "we will not stand for this nonsense."

"Hey, kid," Shane yelled as loud as he could, "there's a ten-foot swamp monster around here. If he gets you, he'll chew off your ears!"

Only the chattering of birds replied.

"Something has happened to him," Janet began to sob. "Oh, Thomas, why did you suggest coming on this bayou trip? It was *your* idea!"

"You liked the idea, too," Thomas Cochran argued. "You were the one who said we should take a boat trip. I wanted to play golf!"

"Golf! How can you talk about golf at a time like this?" Janet continued to sob.

"Will you guys please shut up?" Shane pleaded. "I'm trying to think where a brat like him might have gone."

Shane noticed two small tennis shoe prints near a pond filled with water lilies. He followed the tennis shoe prints along the edge of the pond. Could Robbie have fallen in? A chill went through Shane. He wanted to paddle the kid over his knee, but now the thought that something bad had happened to him chilled his soul.

Shane was responsible for these people. When Captain Thunder signed him on, he'd said sternly, "Now ye remember this, lad. You're first mate. I wouldn't take on any ordinary sixteen-year-old boy. Ah, no. You have a head on your shoulders, lad. It's a heavy task to be first mate to Captain Thunder. You have the responsibility for the folks, same as I do."

Shane dropped to his knees at the side of the pond and stared into the gray water. He saw lizards and tadpoles and leeches, but no sign of Robbie. He scrambled to his feet and ran along the pond, following a deep footprint that led into a dense patch of trees. An underground stream ran this way. Shane knew the bayou country well enough to fear that there might be quicksand in the water ahead. Robbie could have been running after a butterfly. He might have never seen the grassy water until he was sinking.

Quicksand could be a death trap to a frightened child who struggled against it.

"Robbie!" Shane yelled as he fought his way through the vines. The shrieks of birds answered.

"Robbie! Can you hear me?"

Chapter 8

As Shane reached the marsh, a low growl startled him. He was staring at a small wildcat. Once again Shane's blood ran cold. Maybe Robbie was alone here and the wildcat attacked him! After a second, the wildcat wheeled around and streaked off.

"He almost ate me," came a small, shaken voice.

Shane looked up into a tree where Robbie stared down with wide eyes. "I found some Indian arrowheads. Then I saw that big old lion, and I climbed up here," Robbie said.

Relief swept over Shane. He was too glad to be mad. "The cat could have followed you. They climb, you know."

"You came along and scared him off," Robbie said. He looked at Shane almost with admiration.

"Come on down now." Shane said.

"Can't. It's too far down. I'm scared," Robbie said.

"Yeah, I see what you mean," Shane said with a grin he couldn't help. He took the rope hanging from his belt and threw it over the lowest branch of the oak. He hauled himself up, climbing up the branches until he reached Robbie. "You sure climbed way up, kid."

"Yeah. I was scared."

"Climb on my back and hang on for dear life, okay?" Shane commanded. The boy quickly obeyed.

Shane climbed down the tree with the help of his rope, and soon they were down on the shaky earth. He stooped and let Robbie down.

"Why is the ground like jelly?" Robbie asked.

"Because we're standing on water

and just a thin little layer of plants. The ground we're standing on is floating," Shane said. He grasped the boy's hand. "Come on now. Your folks are going nuts with worry."

"Robbie!" both Cochrans screamed when Shane came out of the trees with the boy. Robbie ran to them, his words tumbling over one another. "I almost got eaten by a lion, but Shane scared him away. Shane just looked that old lion in the eye and made him go away. Look, I got some neat arrowheads from the Indians."

Tom Cochran came over to shake Shane's hand. Janet put a tearful kiss on Shane's cheek. Shane turned scarlet and wiped it off.

"Let's go," Shane said gruffly. "We've wasted too much time already. I don't think anybody wants to spend the *night* in this swamp!"

They marched after Shane in single file. Mabel Stanton was right behind

Shane, and she asked, "Did you grow up around here, Shane?"

"Yes ma'am. We live on a bayou just like this one. We have a dock right in front of the house. My brothers and I lie on our stomachs and watch the wild birds and deer, even bears sometimes," Shane said.

"My goodness," Mabel said.

"We have about another hour to walk, and then we'll get to the old house," Shane said. "You folks can stay there until I get the ranger to bring a swamp buggy. He'll have you back to civilization in no time."

"What old house?" Janet Cochran asked.

"We passed it this morning. The old plantation house," Shane said.

"Neato!" Robbie chirped, "that's the old haunted house where the ghosts live. I hope we get to see a real ghost. That would be better than Indian arrowheads!"

"I don't want to stay in a house that's haunted," Janet said in a trembling voice.

"No, no," Shane groaned. "It's not *really* haunted!"

Chapter 9

"You cannot leave us," Janet said, digging her fingers into Shane's arm as she clutched him. "You cannot abandon us in some dreadful haunted house. You're all that stands between us and unspeakable horrors!"

"Look," Shane said, "I made up that story about the house being haunted. It's like show business, see? Captain Thunder taught me to tell wild stories to entertain people."

"You're the only man we have to protect us!" Janet cried. "Tom is no help in a situation like this. He goes to pieces when the kitchen drain gets clogged!"

"Thanks a lot!" Tom Cochran

fumed.

"Daddy's a wimp," Robbie said, laughing.

"Look," Shane said, "when we get to the house, we'll go through all the rooms and make sure it's not haunted. Then I'll race to the ranger, and you'll be back in your nice motel before the sun goes down."

A few times Shane's little group sank into the mud, and clouds of gnats tormented them as they snaked through the marsh. But by late afternoon the old house loomed like a ship in the mists.

"Ugh! It's dreadful!" Janet Cochran said with a shudder.

"I imagine it was once a lovely home for a gentle antebellum family," Mabel sighed.

"How do you know their names were Antebellum?" Robbie asked.

Mabel laughed. "Dear child, antebellum means before the Civil War."

What's the Sibil War?" Robbie demanded.

"Never mind," Shane growled. He was too tired to go into a history lesson. He had to convince Janet Cochran that it was safe to stay here in the house. Then he could dash for the ranger station and finish this nightmare. Shane could run through the swamp like a deer, but with this bunch of tourists on his back he had to creep like a turtle!

"I won't put a foot in that horrible house," Janet insisted as they stood before the rotting porch. Once beautiful columns were now covered with tangled vines. You almost expected a swarm of bats to fly from the broken windows at any moment.

"Okay," Shane said, forcing a grin to his face, "this is what we'll do. The Stanton sisters will go in with me and inspect the house for ghosts. Are you ready, ladies? It looks like it's up to us to convince the Cochrans."

"I'll go in and look for ghosts," Robbie offered. His mother grabbed him and held him tightly.

"Of course," Mabel said. "I'm an educated woman. I certainly don't expect to find a creaky old ghost in there."

"Nor do I," said Ethel with a chuckle.

"All right!" Shane said brightly. He led the way up the groaning porch steps. The front door opened with impressive squeaking. Mabel laughed shakily. "My goodness, just like in a horror movie!" she giggled.

Once inside they saw enormous cobwebs draped over rat-eaten furniture. One large brown rat raced across the floor just ahead of them.

"Gracious!" Ethel said.

"Just a silly little rodent," Mabel chuckled.

A magnificent spiral staircase led upstairs.

"Watch your step, ladies," Shane warned. "Hold on to the railings."

Halfway up the stairs they heard the distinct sound of rattling chains. "How strange," Mabel said in a tight little voice. Then, from the top of the stairs came a long, wailing howl.

Chapter 10

Shane wanted to keep his cool, but he couldn't. He spun around and went racing down the stairs with the Stanton sisters. He never saw old ladies run so fast. They even outran him, and he was going *fast*.

"It's ... unearthly!" Mabel gasped as they rushed into the sunlight.

"It sounded at least half-human," Ethel whispered. She was trembling all over.

"Let's just get out of here," Shane said.

"Did you guys see a ghost?" Robbie demanded.

"We heard a werewolf, I think," Mabel said.

"Neato!" Robbie cried. "I wish I'd been in there!"

"Or maybe a vampire," Ethel said.

Or, Shane thought bitterly, maybe old Captain Thunder. It'd be just like that old scoundrel to hide out in that house and scare people away! But Shane knew it was a lost cause to get his tourists to wait at the house now. He had to push on with the group and hope they got out before nightfall.

The column led by Shane marched though the cypress swamp along the bayou. At least there was no chance of getting lost, because they could follow the river.

"Look at that big old log up ahead," Robbie said as the sun began to set. He broke from his father's grasp and ran to jump on the log. Shane dashed after him, grabbing his shoulder before he leaped onto the sleeping alligator. Startled by the noise, the huge gator slipped into the river with a loud splash.

"Wow!" Robbie gasped, "I almost rode a gator!"

Robbie soon tired, and his father had to carry him. The Stanton sisters slowed down, too. Shane wished desperately for a boat to appear on the river. He could yell to it, and they'd all jump aboard. But the river remained empty and silent except for the loud voices of the frogs and the night birds.

With each step their feet seemed to sink into the mushy earth. Once Mabel went down completely and had to be pulled from a muddy bog.

"Shane," Ethel whispered as Mabel lagged behind, "you can tell me the truth. Do you think we'll make it? My sister is exhausted. She's two years older than I am, you know. And poor Janet is asleep on her feet."

"We'll make it," Shane said. "We're almost to the dock."

"Are you sure?" Mabel asked.

Shane stared out at the black and white world. Black trees stood in blackish water. The trees seemed to be floating above the water. The water and the sky seemed to join together. He couldn't be sure where the sky ended and the water began. Maybe the swamp was playing tricks on Shane. Maybe he wasn't as close to the dock as he thought.

"I'm sure," Shane lied, forcing a smile to his face. That was what a man ought to do, he thought. He had to be strong when strength was needed. He had to act brave so other people could take courage even when his knees trembled with doubt.

They rounded a corner, and Shane let out a cry of joy, "Lights! The dock!" He screamed so loud that he woke Robbie. The boy had been sleeping, his head resting on his father's shoulder.

The ranger sent for cabs to take the tourists back to their motel. The

Cochrans hugged Shane, and Janet stuffed something in his pocket. The Stantons hugged Shane, too, and everybody exchanged addresses. Shane promised to tell the ranger the whole story in the morning, but now he had to get home.

He climbed on his bike and pedaled towards home, only a few blocks away. A big grin touched his face as the night wind freshened him. The Cochrans had given him an envelope. It contained one of Robbie's arrowheads and a one-hundred-dollar bill.

Shane wondered how hard it would be to repair that old boat. If Captain Thunder had disappeared, why maybe Captain Shane could take her down the bayou for the tourists. It wouldn't be a bad way to spend a summer—or maybe a lifetime!